THE INCREDIBLE SHRINKING SQUAD!

by Lucy Rosen
illustrated by Dario Brizuela
inks by Andres Ponce • coloring by Franco Riesco

LITTLE, BROWN & COMPANY
LB kids

Attention,
all Super Hero Squad fans!
Look for these items when you read this book.
Can you spot them all?

DIAMOND

NECKLACE

MONKEY

PRAIRIE DOG

It is a quiet day
in Super Hero City.
Spider-Man, Ant-Man, and Wasp
are bored.

They walk by a jewelry store.
"Let us go in," says Wasp.
"I want to look at necklaces."
Spider-Man and Ant-Man shrug.
They follow her in.

"I need a necklace to match an outfit that I made," she tells her friends.

8

"Oh yeah?" snarls a nasty voice.

It is MODOK!

He and Enchantress

are robbing the store!

The heroes lunge at the villains, but Enchantress yells, "Freeze!" She uses mind control to stop them in their tracks.

"Let us scram," Enchantress says.
She jumps into MODOK's
flying chair as he blasts a hole
through the wall.

Ant-Man, Wasp, and Spider-Man
snap out of their daze.
"Give those back," says Spider-Man.
He shoots a web at MODOK's chair.

"As you wish," laughs MODOK.
He drops the jewels
as he and Enchantress zoom off.
The heroes cannot catch all of them.

Back at headquarters,
Spider-Man explains what happened.
Iron Man looks at a scan of the area.

"Looks like the jewels fell into the zoo," says Iron Man.

"A ruby ring landed near the monkeys.

A necklace is in the birdhouse.

And a big diamond is in a prairie dog den.

We will have to get past the animals."

The heroes hurry to the zoo.
"I will take the monkeys,"
says Spider-Man.
"Wasp, you take the birds.
Ant-Man, you get the prairie dogs."

16

At the monkey house,
Spider-Man quickly sees the ring.
He reaches out, but a monkey grabs it!
"Quit monkeying around!"
yells Spider-Man.

Over at the birdhouse,

Wasp searches for the necklace.

"Oh no," she cries.

A bird is tucking it into the nest!

Ant-Man is also having trouble.
A prairie dog has the diamond,
but the animal dives into its hole!
"Get back here!" shouts Ant-Man.

"What are we going to do?" asks Wasp.
"We cannot grab the jewels
without the animals seeing us."
"I have a tiny idea!" says Ant-Man.

"Hold tight, everybody," he says.
He uses his powers
to shrink them all down to bug size!
"See if the animals spy us now!"

Spider-Man rushes back to see
that the monkey still has the ring.
"Time to go bananas,"
jokes Spider-Man.

He spins a web so thin that
the monkey does not see it.
The animal swings right into it,
and Spider-Man grabs the ruby ring.

Back inside the birdhouse,

Wasp flies up to the nest.

She searches among the twigs.

"Got it!" cries Wasp
when she finds the necklace.
She jumps on the bird's back
to catch a flight down.
The bird never notices a thing!

Ant-Man jumps into the prairie dog hole. The big, shiny diamond is in the den, but Ant-Man is now too small to lift it!

"Care to lend some hands?"
he calls out to his friends.
Spider-Man and Wasp
help him carry out the diamond.

Ant-Man returns all three of them
to normal size.
"We did it!" the heroes shout.
"Not exactly," growls a familiar voice.
Enchantress and MODOK are back!

"We want to keep the jewels after all,"
Enchantress says.
"How nice of you to get them for us."
Ant-Man, Spider-Man, and Wasp
know just what to do.

Ant-Man shrinks the other heroes again.

"What is going on here?"

asks MODOK in surprise.

Wasp buzzes around the bad guys.

"Stop that noise!" they cry.

Enchantress and MODOK

try to run away,

but Spider-Man traps them in a web!

"Nice job, guys," says Ant-Man.
"Looks like teamwork
comes in all sizes!"

Bates

WELCOME TO
PASSPORT TO READING
A beginning reader's ticket to a brand-new world!

Every book in this program is designed to build read-along and read-alone skills, level by level, through engaging and enriching stories. As the reader turns each page, he or she will become more confident with new vocabulary, sight words, and comprehension.

These PASSPORT TO READING levels will help you choose the perfect book for every reader.

READING TOGETHER
Read short words in simple sentence structures together to begin a reader's journey.

READING OUT LOUD
Encourage developing readers to sound out words in more complex stories with simple vocabulary.

READING INDEPENDENTLY
Newly independent readers gain confidence reading more complex sentences with higher word counts.

READY TO READ MORE
Readers prepare for chapter books with fewer illustrations and longer paragraphs.

This book features sight words from the educator-supported Dolch Sight Word List. Readers will become more familiar with these commonly used vocabulary words, increasing reading speed and fluency.

For more information, please visit www.passporttoreadingbooks.com, where each reader can add stamps to a personalized passport while traveling through story after story!

Enjoy the journey!

Little, Brown and Company

Hachette Book Group
237 Park Avenue, New York, NY 10017
Visit our website at www.lb-kids.com

LB kids is an imprint of Little, Brown and Company. The LB kids name and logo
are trademarks of Hachette Book Group, Inc.

The publisher is not responsible for websites (or their content)
that are not owned by the publisher.

First Edition: April 2012

ISBN 978-0-316-17862-4

Library of Congress Control Number: 2011935090

10 9 8 7 6 5 4 3 2 1

CW

Printed in the United States of America